THE RETURN OF
CUCHULAIN

BY

EIMAR O'DUFFY

British Library Cataloguing-in-Publication Data
A catalogue record for this book is available from
the British Library

Contents

EIMAR O'DUFFY

Eimar O'Duffy was born in Dublin in 1893. He was educated at Stonyhurst College, Lancashire, and University College, Dublin, where he became interested in Irish cultural and political nationalism. He began publishing in his twenties, producing his first novel, *The Wasted Island,* in 1919. This early work, which examined critically the origins of the 1916 Easter Uprising in Ireland, exhibited the sharp satirical style – and scepticism towards the political direction of his native country – for which he was to become known.

Much like other Irish writers such as James Joyce and Brinsley McNamara, O'Duffy's expression of his disillusionment with Ireland gained him as many detractors as it did fans. In 1925, having lost his job at Department of External Affairs in Dublin as a result of his outspoken views, he emigrated to England. Here, between 1926 and 1933, he produced his Cuandine trilogy, the works for which he is best remembered. A scathing, Swiftian denouncement of the ills of global capitalism and debt culture (O'Duffy was also an astute economist), the trilogy – made up of *King Goshawk and the Birds* (1926), *The Spacious Adventures of the Man in the Street* (1928), and *Asses in Clover* (1933) – is now seen as near-prophetic by some critics, and remains an acclaimed work of satire.

Towards the end of his life, O'Duffy turned his hand to writing detective stories, with mixed success. He also displayed some talent as a literary critic, and was one of the first people to recognize James Joyce's *Ulysses* (1922) as a masterpiece. He died of duodenal ulcers in 1935, at the age of 42.

*　　*　　*

The Philosopher came upon the spirits of the heroes walking in the meadows of asphodel in Tir na nOg. They were not like the spirit of Socrates, which resembled a still flame; but they had the forms of men, glorious and ethereal. A hero is a person of superabundant vitality and predominant will, with no sense of responsibility or humour, which makes him a nuisance on earth; but he is in his element in the third heaven. There the heroes take themselves and one another at their own valuation, regarding their weaknesses as strength, their defects as merits. Their life is in their fame: every time an earthly orator recites their names they experience thrills of pleasure; if they are forgotten they die.

The Philosopher recognised many of the heroes as they walked in golden sunlight over the meadows of asphodel: Hector and Achilles arm in arm; Horatius in friendly colloquy with the Tusculan Mamilius; Henry V. of England; Patrick Sarsfield and Shane O'Neill; Bertrand du Guesclin; Garibaldi; and there were many more whom he did not know, mighty men of every race and nation that has shed blood on the green fields of earth. To none of these did the Philosopher address himself, but ever kept a watch for the one that seemed to him best suited for his purpose: namely, Cuchulain of Muirthemne, son of Dechtire and of Lugh of the Long Hand, of whom it was said in his time that there was none to compare with him for valour and truth, for magnanimity and courtesy, for strength and comeliness among the heroes of the world. In the crowd that went by there was none that resembled him. The Philosopher therefore passed on, and crossing another field he came to a glade, and saw before him a bush spangled with blossoms of ever-changing colours, that played sweet music in the breath of the wind. In the shadow of the bush reposed a youth of exceeding beauty. Three colours were in his hair: brown at the skin, blood-red in the middle, golden at the ends. Snow-white was his skin; as seven jewels was the brightness of his kingly eyes. Seven fingers had he on each hand; seven toes on each foot; and if you doubt it, go straightway and poke your misbelieving nose into the pages of the Book of Leinster or the Book of the Dun

3

Cow or the Yellow Book of Leccan, where all these things are faithfully recorded, with a good deal more that I spare you. Certain it is that it was by these marks that the Philosopher knew that the youth in front of him was Cuchulain.

By the hero's side lay a woman, with her head resting amorously on his shoulder. Very fair she was, with two plaits of hair of the rich hue of marigolds, eyes as blue as the wood anemone, and her naked body as white as the foam of the sea. The Philosopher took her at first to be Emer; but presently in their love talk, which held him entranced as by celestial music, he heard Cuchulain call her Fand; at which the Philosopher was moved to indignant speech. Said he:

'I thought that affair was over since Manannan Mac Lir shook his cloak of forgetfulness between you. And surely it were only just to render to Emer in heaven that faithfulness you denied to her on earth.'

'You forget,' said Cuchulain, 'that in heaven there is no marrying nor giving in marriage. As for this'—looking down at the woman—'I am tired of it,' whereupon he cast her from him, and she vanished. 'She was but the figment of my imagination,' said he, 'made with a wish; unmade with another: for heaven is but the fulfilment of the heart's desire.'

'I do not care for this heaven,' said the Philosopher.

'Your desire is nobler,' said Cuchulain. 'You should seek a higher heaven.'

'I am not a spirit,' said the Philosopher. 'I am the mind of a man, and I have come all the way from Earth to find you.'

'What is your errand?' asked Cuchulain.

'Man,' said the Philosopher, 'is full of wickedness and folly.'

'True,' said Cuchulain. 'Tell me what wickedness and folly he has done since I left the earth.'

'In the first place,' said the Philosopher, 'he is never done fighting and killing.'

'That,' said Cuchulain, 'is foolish, but it is not wicked. I fought and killed many in my time on earth. I am since convinced of folly, but I am clear of guilt.'

'In those days,' said the mind of the Philosopher, 'men fought with men in hot blood, hand to hand, strength against strength, feat against feat, and knowing well what it was they were fighting for. But for many centuries they have been possessed of a devilish

4

powder which enables them to kill at a distance; and by labouring hard at its improvement they have learnt how to kill without seeing one another at all. So that now when countries are at war they do not send forth armies, but each hurls millions of missiles over mountains and seas at the other, destroying lands and cities, men, women, and children, until one or other is utterly overwhelmed. Some of these missiles are so cunningly devised that when they hit they divide up into thousands of particles which riddle and macerate the body; others contain deadly poisons; others scatter the contagion of leprosy and such foul diseases through the air; others on bursting are converted into a fine dust which is borne on the wind and blinds every eye in which it finds lodgement. They inflict on each other besides a thousand more abominations of which I cannot tell you, for already I grow weaker and must soon yield to the earthward pull of my body. But you must know this also, that nobody ever knows the real cause or meaning of these wars, and that if any one asks he is immediately put to silence.'

Said the spirit of Cuchulain: 'This is indeed a most iniquitous way of fighting. But is the tale of man's wickedness and folly complete?'

'No,' said the Philosopher. 'That is only the beginning. While the many are thus fighting, the few are contriving against their liberties, and robbing them of their bread and their homes, so that all the wealth of the world has now passed into the hands of usurers. And at last, infamy of infamies, these have begun to covet the beauty of the world as well.' Then he told Cuchulain of the bird-purchase of King Goshawk; and at that the hero was thrown into a rage surpassing even that of Socrates.

'Enough!' said he. 'I will rest here no longer. Let us to earth at once.'

*　　*　　*

So the Philosopher's mind returned to him in the little room in the back lane off Stoneybatter; and having rubbed his natural eyes he saw the spirit of Cuchulain standing before him, glorious and resplendent as a flame in a dark place, as a fountain among stagnant waters.

'Welcome to Earth and to my humble abode,' said the Philosopher. 'And pray pardon me if I leave you for a moment: for I

5

must find you a body, in order that you may go inconspicuously among men, and see for yourself the folly and wickedness from which you would redeem them.' And at that he took himself off, leaving the hero gazing in bewilderment at the strange habitation of the heir of the ages.

Now there was a man dwelling on the same floor as the Philosopher who thought life was not worth living; for he had to spend most of it making up pounds and half-pounds of tea, sugar, flour, butter, cheese, bacon, sausages, and the like into parcels, and being polite to the fools that bought them; and he had to subsist himself on the same commodities, which he hated with the same intensity and for the same reason as the slaves who built the Pyramids must have hated the architecture of Ancient Egypt. He felt that it was no life for a man to rise in the morning before the sun had taken the chill from the air, to be at every one's beck and call during the best hours of the day, and not to be free till its tag end when there was nothing to do but sit in a stuffy picturehouse puffing fags. Of course there were also Saturday afternoons and Sundays: but what could you do with a half-day beyond killing time at the pictures or a football match? and most of a Sunday was gone by the time you had heard Mass and finished dinner, and the picture-houses didn't open till eight o'clock. Oh, it was a hard life and a dull life to be doomed to, very different from the life of his dreams. He would have liked to be rich, to be exquisitely dressed, to live in a gorgeous house, to have abundance of leisure, to have silent, smoothlygliding servants and automobiles always at his command, to be loved and won by glorious shining women— in short, to live like the heroes of his favourite film dramas. Instead of that he had to work, to obey orders, to loiter aimlessly between whiles, to wear cheap ready-made suits, to dodge other people's motors and serve their servants with sugar and sausages, and every hour of the day to be tempted by the sight of women customers and passers-by with pretty ankles and swelling hips and bosoms, that would stir up hot tormenting passions which he could only satisfy by risking damnation to eternal brimstone, or else by getting married—which he couldn't afford, and besides the girl he was walking out with was no great marvel, with her pale lips and her flat chest and her thin legs that didn't properly fill her stockings. Oh, a very dull life, thought Mr Robert Emmett Aloysius O'Kennedy.

It was to this man that the Philosopher came seeking the loan of a body. He was standing before his mirror wondering whether he ought to wash his neck that morning when he heard the Philosopher's knock.

'Come in and sit down,' he said hospitably, for he liked the Philosopher, thinking him an amusing old ass. 'You don't mind if I go on washing?' he added. 'Because I'll be late if I don't,' and, having decided to spare his neck for yet another day, he began vigorously to sponge his face.

'You told me the other day,' said the Philosopher, 'that you didn't consider life worth living.'

'I did,' said Mr O'Kennedy.

'Do you still think the same?' asked the Philosopher.

'I do,' said Mr O'Kennedy, and began to dry his face in an exceedingly dirty towel.

'Would you like to quit it for a time?' asked the Philosopher.

'I'd like to quit it for good,' said Mr O'Kennedy emphatically.

'For ever is a long time,' said the Philosopher. 'But I think we could manage a month.'

Mr O'Kennedy would have winked here if there had been anybody to wink at. The old boy was certainly more cracked than usual this morning.

'What is your body worth?' asked the Philosopher.

'Couldn't be sure,' said Mr O'Kennedy. 'The boss pays me three quid a week for the use of it, but I think he includes my soul in the bargain.'

'Your body is all I want,' said the Philosopher. 'What do you say to two pounds ten? And while I'm using it your soul can go off to heaven for a rest.'

'Done,' said Mr O'Kennedy, who thought he had a yarn that would keep his friends in stitches for a week.

Then the Philosopher put Mr O'Kennedy sitting in a chair; and he made three passes with his hands; at which the body of the young man became fixed and immovable, and his soul was filled with fear.

'Stop!' he cried. 'You are killing me.'

'You said that was what you wanted,' said the Philosopher.

'I didn't mean it,' said Mr O'Kennedy.

Then the Philosopher made three more passes; and the soul of the young man departed from him, and went wandering into space.

7

But the Philosopher took his body, and stripped it, and washed it thoroughly, and brought it to his own room, where he set it down before Cuchulain, saying:

'Come, now. Here is a body: a poor thing; a pitiful thing; not too well made, and somewhat marred in use; but still a semblable human body. Put it on.'

Cuchulain looked at the body and did not like it at all; for it was meanly shaped, without sign of beauty or strength. The muscles were small and flabby; the spine curved; the feet distorted fantastically by ill-fitting boots: a body unsuited to a hero. Cuchulain picked it up distastefully, as one might handle another's soiled combinations. Then he gave it a shake and clasped it to him; the spirit seemed to melt and blend with the body; and presently the heart of Robert Emmett Aloysius O'Kennedy began to beat, his lungs to breathe, his eyes to open, and his limbs to stretch themselves, as if the soul within were testing its new tenement. For some minutes after the figure stood motionless, with introspective eyes, like one in contemplation. Then came a lightning change: convulsions seized upon the body of Mr O'Kennedy, and in an instant Cuchulain had cast it from him with a cry of horror.

'O pitiful brain of man,' he said. 'What fears, what habits, what ordinances, what prohibitions have stamped you slave. I thought just now that I was in a very sweat of terror of some dreadful being named the Boss, who held over me mysterious powers, and from whom I anticipated chastisement if I were late in his service today, as I most assuredly expected to be. At the same time I felt a certain small satisfaction in remembering that yesterday I had done him some underhand injury which he would be unable to trace to my account. It was but a small weed of joy in a forest of fears. I had a fear that a man I knew might have heard that I had spoken ill of him that day; and another fear that a man I had lied to might find me out. I had also a fear that my clothes were not quite the same as were worn by every one else, and a fear of what all the people I knew might be saying or thinking of me at the moment. Then there was in me a fear that had been inspired some time ago by a play I had seen, which made me seem to myself a mean, stupid, and malicious creature; and of that fear there was born in me a hatred of the play and of the man who wrote it. I hated him for using the theatre, where I went to enjoy myself, as a means of making me hate myself. And that recalled to my memory the worst fear of all those that beset me. For in the same theatre a few days before I had watched some women dancing, and my eyes had feasted on the roundness of their limbs, and my body had been bathed in warm desires. For that sin I was damned eternally to a pit of flame unless I should repent and confess. I was afraid to confess, for fear of what the druid should think of me: and I was afraid not to confess for fear of the pit of flame. Then I began to make excuses for myself, saying that I had not looked very long and that after all there had not been much to see, so that I had not sinned mortally, and had earned only some temporary fire. But I could not make myself feel quite sure of that; nor could I decide whether I was more afraid of the confession or the pit of fire. Then I began to wonder whether there was really a God or a pit of fire at all. But I dared not let myself think of that, lest I should be struck dead and buried in the pit of fire forthwith: whereupon I—even I, Cuchulain—was seized with a loathsome terror, to escape which I cast the foul body from me. And let you, O Philosopher, remove it now; for I swear by the sunlight of Tir na nOg that I will not take to me such a horror again.'

'That is not spoken like Cuchulain,' replied the Philosopher, 'who in the olden times, when he was a man and a hero, was never known to look back from a task that he had once undertaken. It is clear, however, that the spirit is affected by the condition of the somatic substrate on which it depends for expression, so I will clean it up and let you try it on again.'

So saying the Philosopher took scalpel and forceps, and, having opened the skull of Robert Emmett Aloysius O'Kennedy, and carefully reflected the membranes, he exposed the brain to the full glare of the morning sun. Then in a bottle he compounded a lotion of carbolic acid, cold horse sense, and common soap, with which he thoroughly scoured and irrigated both the psychical centres of the cerebral cortex and the association fibres connecting them with each other and with the sensory centres: for, as Halliburton or another hath it, *Nihil est in intellectu quod non prius in sensu fuerit*. After this operation, Cuchulain entered again into the body, which straightway began to glow with a divine beauty. The skin glistened like white satin; great muscles swelled and rippled beneath it; the chest expanded to a third as much again as it was; the back straightened like a spring released; the eyes

9

flashed fire; and the sheepish countenance of Robert Emmett Aloysius O'Kennedy shone like that of a hero in his feats. Again Cuchulain began to test the strength of his borrowed frame, stretching the arms above his head, expanding the chest, stamping the feet on the ground: until at last the Philosopher cried:

'Hold now! Enough! Do you not remember all the war-chariots and the swords and spears you broke in the testing the day you first took arms and went foraying against the Dun of Nechtan's sons? This bag of bones is too frail for such experimenting, and if you wreck it I cannot get you another. Besides it is only hired by the week.'

Then sounded the voice of Cuchulain from the vocal chords of Robert Emmett Aloysius O'Kennedy like a symphony of Beethoven from the brass trumpet of a cheap gramophone, saying: 'Excellent advice, O Sage, and none too soon, for already I feel my shoulders crack. I will forbear in other respects, but the ghosts of my seven toes are most uncomfortably crammed into the warped and etiolated extremities of this starveling here, so that I seem to tread on dried peas: therefore stretch them I must.' So he sat down, and began bunching his toes as one might do to expand a shrunken stocking; and with the effort the metatarsal bones straightened out, the phalanges uncurled, a shower of corns and bunions fell on the floor, and the two feet, which had hitherto looked more like the bleached rhizomes of some unknown plant than any part of an intelligent animal, assumed a healthy shape and hue, and heroic proportions. Even so Cuchulain was not yet comfortable in his corporeal tenement, but presently said to the Philosopher, very wry in the face: 'I fear I can never wed myself peaceably to this flesh. Lo, I have here'—pointing to his belly—'a most woeful and disturbing sensation, as of a griping emptiness, and unless it is soon relieved I will abandon this carnal vesture yet again and return to Tir na nOg.'

'That is most unfortunate,' said the Philosopher. 'I had hoped you would be free of the human frailties and the physical needs which hamper us. This pain you feel is called hunger, and it is the prick of the goad with which King Flesh reminds us that we are his slaves, forcing us to cram ourselves with bread and meat, which we metabolise into energy, which we must use to procure more bread and meat, thus remaining in a vicious circle of uselessness, eating to live and living to eat, instead of turning our minds to the pursuit of wisdom. And now that I come to think of it, I am hungry myself, and no wonder, for I have forgotten how long it is since my last meal. Have patience now, and in a moment both our pangs shall be assuaged.'

The Philosopher then went out, and in a shop at the corner of the street he bought a loaf of bread, a piece of cheese, and a quart of milk; on which provender he and Cuchulain fared right joyously, charging their batteries with peptone and the other approved albuminoids, not forgetting a due proportion of vitamins as prescribed by the medical columns of the Sunday papers. Believe me, bread and cheese and milk is the best food in the world for hungry men, when you can trust your dairyman and beer is under a ban: the proof of which is that when Cuchulain had finished he rose from his chair, and, stretching himself, put a foot through the floor and both hands through the ceiling.

'Steady!' said the Philosopher. 'This is not Bricriu's Palace. It is time your limbs were fettered with the garments of civilised society.' So saying, he took out some spare ones of his own and showed Cuchulain how to put them on. Be sure that Cuchulain in donning the trousers and tucking in the shirt showed no more grace or dignity than your mortal man—poet, priest, politician, soldier, average fool, or father of ten. I wish, indeed, that all men who hold position or notoriety could be compelled to put on their trousers publicly at least once a year: by which means we should rid ourselves of a vast quantity of that humbug and hero-worship which make the world intolerable for honest and self-reliant men. For, as the proverb says, no man is a hero to his valet: the reason being that the valet sees the hero getting into his trousers.

*   *   *

Thus clothed and fed, Cuchulain set forth with the Philosopher to explore the city. What a sight was here for eyes accustomed to the splendours of Tir na nOg. Come, O Muse, whoever you be, that stood by the elbow of immortal Zola, take this pen of mine and pump it full of such foul and fetid ink as shall describe it worthily. To what shall I compare it? A festering corpse, maggot-crawling, under a carrion-kissing sun? A loathly figure, yet insufficient: for your maggot thrives on corruption, and grows sleeker with the progression of putridity (O happy maggot, whom the dross of the world trammels not, had you but an immortal soul how surely would it aspire heavenward!). But your lord of creation rots with his environment; so the true symbol of our city is a carrion so pestilent that it corrupts its own maggots.

What ruin and decay were here: what filth and litter: what nauseating stenches. The houses were so crazy with age and so shaken with bombardments that there was scarce one that could stand without assistance: therefore they were held together by plates and rivets, or held apart by cross-beams, or braced up by scaffoldings, so that the street had the appearance of a dead forest. (Was it not a strange perversity that slew the living tree to lengthen the days of these tottering skeletons?) Many of the houses were roofless; others were inhabited only in their lower storeys; some had collapsed altogether, and squatters had built them huts of wood or mud or patchwork on the hard-pounded rubble. The streets were ankle-deep in dung and mire; craters yawned in their midst; piles of wrecked masonry obstructed them. Rivulets ran where the gutters had been. Foul sewer smells issued from holes and cracks.

Fit lairage was this for the tragomaschaloid mob that jostled the celestial visitor to the realms of earth. What stink of breath and body assailed his nostrils; what debased accents, raucous voices, and evil language offended his hearing; what grime, what running sores, what raw-rimmed eye-sockets, what gum-suppuration and tooth-rot, what cavernous cheeks, what leering lips and hopeless eyes, what pain-twisted faces, what sagging spines, what streeling steps, what filthy ragged raiment covering what ghastly-imagined hideousness of body sickened his beauty-nurtured sight.

Yet with all this putridity and squalor there were not wanting, even in those bygone days, many signs of progress and private enterprise. At every street corner there were loud-speakers which yelled forth news and advertisements. Airplanes circled like great dragon-flies in the sky, squirting out smoke-signals such as: 'Read Cumbersome's Papers', 'Why have a Bad Leg? Try Popham's Pills', 'Trust the Trusts that Feed You', 'Vote for Coddo', '*To him that hath shall be given*. Scripture backs the Trusts', 'Are you Languid? Try Peppo'. But these were but superficial signs of civilisation. If the hero had taken the pains to inquire, he would have learnt that every foot of land in the neighbourhood was worth fabulous sums of money; and that by a miracle of organisation every square inch of rag on the backs of the people, and every crust fermenting in their bellies had helped to make millions for somebody. Cuchulain, however, was too preoccupied with the uglier side of things to make any such inquiries. Was he not a morbid ghoul and gloomy pessimist thus to nose and grope in the dark for hidden horrors, with the best of life dancing before him in the warm sunshine?

In the pother and hurly-burly I have described, owing to the celestial vigour of Cuchulain, which was chafed rather than impaired by his catatheosis, and to the enfeeblement of the Philosopher, in whom the milk and cheese had not yet replenished the loss of tissue occasioned by his fast, the two became separated, Cuchulain pursuing his way alone, and the Philosopher, after a vain attempt to overtake him, returning to his lodging. Cuchulain, however, not perceiving the loss of his companion, strode onward with more than earthly vigour, to the grave detriment of his borrowed body, which was thereby shaken up, loosened, and derivetted, like a cheap car fitted with a too powerful engine, so that soon the stomach of Robert Emmett Aloysius O'Kennedy began to clamour for more nutriment.

Just as this clamour was beginning to be unbearable, Cuchulain espied a shop window most alluringly arrayed, with a cargo more varied and of more diverse origins than ever was carried by Venetian argosy or Corinthian trireme or galley of Tyre or ancient Sidon. There were oranges there from Jaffa and Seville, and little golden tangerines from Africa nestling in silver tinfoil. There were lemons from Italy and Spain; olives and currants from the land of Hellas; raisins from the Levant, and sultanas and muscatels. Figs were there from Smyrna, and dates from Morocco, Tripoli, and Cyrenaica; bananas, the long straight kind, from Jamaica, and short curved ones from the Canaries; and pineapples and cocoanuts from the islands whose palm-trees fan the Pacific. Then there were cheeses of a hundred species: great Stiltons like mouldy casks from a tangle of jetsam; Gorgonzola streaked like marble; rich yellow English Gloucester; Dutch cheeses like bloated beetroots; hygienic cheeses done up in jars to keep in the vitamines; evanescent-flavoured Gruyère and sharp-fanged Roquefort; simple chaste Cheddar, and sensuous Camembert. There were teas also from China, India, and Ceylon, coffee from the East

Indies, cocoa from Brazil and Ecuador, and sugar from five continents and a hundred isles. Rice was there from many lands—China and Japan, Persia and Siam; and with it were pearly sago and slippery tapioca. There were tinned sardines there from France and Scotland; tinned salmon and potted meat from America. From Canada there was shredded wheat and macaroni; and macaroni also from Italy. Great pyramids of apples there were, from England and from the home orchards: some red as the blush of a country maiden, some yellow like shining taffety; with pale Newtown pippins and quiet green baking apples. Over all hung fine well-smoked hams and bacon flitches from Denmark (with a few from Limerick), and American bacon like greasy tallow. And there were biscuits and chocolates and candied fruits and nuts and odds and ends from the Lord knows where. All these things came as tribute to the men of Eirinn: they made nothing for themselves.

Here, therefore, Cuchulain turned in that he might find the wherewithal to appease the revolt of the baser nature he had put on; but he had scarce set foot in the shop before he was accosted by a large and ferocious person with stand-up hair and waxed moustaches, who, hauling him forward by the lapel of his coat, bawled into his face: 'What's the meaning of this, you blasted young slacker? An hour late! You can leave this day week; and go behind the counter this minute and make up the orders or I'll smash your face in.'

'Sir,' said Cuchulain, 'I know not what your rank is, nor what you take me for. Howbeit, I am not used to being handled thus, or being spoken to in such fashion as you have assailed me withal. Loose me, therefore, lest the grossness of this body which I am wrapped in should foul my spirit with thoughts of anger.'

The Manager, however, had not in all his life been conscious of the image of God in any shop boy: neither were his eyes opened now. Therefore, taking a stronger hold of Cuchulain, he would have thrust him ignominiously before him, had not the hero, by a sudden exertion of his muscles, maintained himself as if rooted to the floor.

'Come on, now, you obstinate young devil!' cried the Manager, giving him a flip on the ear with his great fat hand.

Anger came on Cuchulain at that, and a terrible appearance came over him. Each hair of his head stood on end, with a drop of blood at its tip. One of his eyes started forth a hand's-breadth out of its socket, and the other was sucked down into the depths of his breast. His whole body was contorted. His ribs parted asunder, so that there was room for a man's foot between them; his calves and his buttocks came round to the front of his body. At the same time the hero-light shone around his head, and the Bocanachs and Bananachs and the Witches of the Valley raised a shout around him. For such was his appearance when his anger was upon him; as testify the Yellow Book of Leccan and the other chronicles; which, if any man doubt, let him search his conscience whether he have not believed even stranger things printed in newspapers. For myself, I think the chroniclers are the more trustworthy, as they are certainly the more entertaining; for, if they lie, they lie for the fun of it, whereas the journalists lie for pay, or through sheer inability to observe or report correctly.

Now when the Manager of MacWhatsisname's grocery saw Cuchulain facing him in the same dreadful guise wherein he overcame Ferdiad at the ford and drove Fergus before him from the field of Gairech, the strength went out of his limbs, and the corpuscles of his blood fled in disgraceful rout to seek refuge in the inmost marrow of his bones. Dreadful were the scenes that were then enacted in the arched and slippery dark purple passages of his venous system. Smitten with a common panic, Red Cells, Lymphocytes, and Phagocytes rushed in headlong confusion down the peripheral veins, which soon became choked with swarming struggling masses of fugitives. Millions of smaller Lymphocytes and Mast Cells perished in the crush, but the immense mobs poured on towards the larger vessels. Yet even here there was no relief: for as each tributary stream ingurgitated its protoplasmic horde, these too became stuffed to suffocation; so that, though every corpuscle strove onward with all his strength, the jammed and stifled cell mass could scarce be seen to move. Here and there bands of armed Phagocytes, impatient of delay, tried to cut themselves a passage through the helpless huddled mass of Lymphocytes and Platelets: but they succeeded only in walling themselves up with impenetrable mounds of slaughtered carcases. Still more frightful scenes occurred when two mobs, travelling by anastomosing vessels, met each other head to head: for while those in front fought in grim despair for possession of the road until it was totally blocked and thrombosed with their bodies, the cells behind, still

15

harried by fear, pressed onward as vigorously as ever, to the great discomfiture of the dense crowds packed between, who, thus driven by an irresistible force against an impenetrable obstacle, perished in millions.

Thus was the Manager's blood very literally curdled. And straightway Cuchulain made his salmon-leap and fisted him a smasher under the third waistcoat button, breaking four of his ribs, and hurling him backwards against the counter with enough force to crack the front of it; yet he was so well covered behind that he took no further hurt, though by his screams you would have thought he had been dumped upon the hob of hell. Then, having wrecked the shop and all it contained, Cuchulain went forth into the street, breaking a thigh or a collar-bone for any that attempted to stop him: for all which he was most soundly rated by the Philosopher when he returned to him at the close of the day.

'What have I done?' said the Philosopher. 'Old footling dunderhead that I am. What have I fetched out of heaven to show mankind his wickedness and folly? Have you no respect for our civilisation that you must sally forth, as fiery-wild as upon that first foray of yours in the barbarous youth of the world, and the first grocer's shop you come to, must leave your sign of hand upon it as though it had been the Dun of Nechtan's sons. This will never do. If two thousand years of heaven have not tamed your soul, you must tame it now; or if it is the body of Mr O'Kennedy that is at fault, then you must bring it into subjection right rapidly: for this sort of thing cannot be done in these days.'

'What,' said Cuchulain, 'have you no such pests now as these sons of Nechtan whose Dun lay athwart the road out of Ulster into Meath, and they took toll of blood and treasure of all that came by? A right strong place it was, not to be easily taken; and the sons of Nechtan were protected by magic also, so that Foill, the eldest, could not be killed with edge of sword or point of lance; and Tuachel, the second, if he were not killed by the first thrust or the first cut, could not be killed at all; and the youngest, Fandall, was swifter in the water than a swallow in the air: yet I slew them all, and gave their Dun to the winds to howl in, and to the wild beasts of Sliabh Fuaith for a lairage. Have you no such pests now?'

'A many!' said the Philosopher. 'Their duns lie across all the ways of the men of Ireland, and none may eat or drink or walk abroad without paying them toll. But they cannot be brought low by such tactics as these: for they are more cunningly fenced in, and protected by more potent magic, than ever were the sons of Nechtan. This Goshawk that I told you of is one of them: and I wish you would learn to control yourself, lest you find yourself in a gaol before you can cross swords with him. But, come now. When you had vindicated your honour by thrashing the grocer, what was your next exploit? Tell me all.'

'When I had left the grocer,' said Cuchulain, 'I walked farther up the street until I came to an eating-house, which I entered very gladly, as I was feeling the pangs of my adopted stomach more keenly than ever. Here I was received at first more courteously than in any other place in this earth of yours. The master of the house bowed low to me, gave me a chair by a table clothed with fine linen, and summoned a servant to attend to my wants. Right generous and goodly fare was then put before me, and I fed full, to the manifest enjoyment of this voracious body. Afterwards, when I had rested me a while, I sought out the master of the house that I might thank him for his hospitality: but in the midst of my speech I was interrupted by the aforesaid servitor, who thrust a piece of paper into my hand, saying, "Your bill, sir," whereat the master of the house said, "Good morning, sir; much obliged; pay at the desk." Then there came upon me a most noble rage, not this time out of the spleen of O'Kennedy, but out of my own soul; and I said: "Pay! Thou kindless, impious, inhospitable boor! What shall I pay?" for I had thought the place to be a hostelry for the free entertainment of strangers, such as they have in all the planets I have ever visited, and as they had in Eirinn in the olden time. Then said my host: "I don't know what part of the world you come from, stranger: but in this benighted country you don't get nothing for nothing." "Very well, then," I said, " I will pay. But not now, since I have not the wherewithal. Good day to you, therefore. I will return anon." So saying, I would have departed in peace, but the fellow laid hand on my shoulder, saying that he would not suffer me to go until I had paid what I owed. By my hand of valour, my word never was doubted before. Therefore I smote him, yet not very hard: only so as to lay him senseless at my feet, but with the life still in him.' (Here the Philosopher groaned.) 'After that,' said Cuchulain, 'two warriors, twins, clad both alike in blue, and their helmets embossed with shining steel, came to his assistance. To these I would willingly have explained the justice of the case, but before I could speak they seized upon me, so that I was compelled to defend myself. Yet, pitying their ignorance, I did them no injury, only binding them back to back with their own harness.'

The Philosopher groaned again, and said: 'How many people altogether have you maimed and killed? Speak out. Let me know the worst at once.'

'Venerable sir,' said Cuchulain, 'I maimed no more; neither did I kill any. After that I went to a picture-house, but seeing that there was a charge for admission, I did not enter. And by my hand of valour, there is no other planet in the universe—not even among the savage seventy that revolve around the Dog Star—that acts so scurvily: for pictures were meant to elevate the soul, and therefore cannot be priced.'

'What a pity you had no money,' said the Philosopher.

'After that,' said Cuchulain, 'I entered a car driven by electricity. What do you call them?' 'Trams.' 'Trams. I thank you. Your trams are tolerable. Nay, I have seen worse, but I have forgotten where. In this tram there were seventeen people, whom I observed with great interest. Nine of them wore discs of glass before their eyes, held in place by a band of metal fixed to the nose. Why did they do that?'

'To enable them to see,' said the Philosopher. 'Their eyes were bad.'

'Why?' asked Cuchulain.

'Civilisation,' said the Philosopher.

'Twelve of them,' said Cuchulain, 'had strange looking teeth of a most unnatural aspect.'

'They were false teeth,' said the Philosopher.

'What became of their own?' asked Cuchulain.

'Rotted,' said the Philosopher.

'Why?' asked Cuchulain.

'Civilisation,' said the Philosopher.

'Ten of them,' said Cuchulain, 'had complexions of a pale green colour, with dull eyes and drooping lips. What was the meaning of this?'

'They were poisoned,' said the Philosopher, 'by eating too much preserved food.'

'Why did they do that?' asked Cuchulain.

'They could afford no better.'

'Why?' asked Cuchulain.

'Civilisation,' said the Philosopher.

'Eight of them,' said Cuchulain, 'had sores on their faces; and there were two that could not sit straight, but balanced themselves tenderly on half a rump. What was wrong with them, venerable sir?'

The Philosopher, with all commendable delicacy, gave explanation of the phenomenon.

Said Cuchulain: 'The bottom of your civilisation is in no better case. Never have I seen so many and such strange diseases as upon this little planet. Yet you have learned and charitable physicians to cure these ills, whose advice was written plain upon the windows of the tram; as, for instance: *Are you jaded, weary, dispirited? Have you that tired feeling? Then try Peppo;* and, *Is your Liver bad? Mixo will set you right;* and again, *You feel well today. But who knows what loathsome diseases the Future may bring in its train? If you want to* KEEP *well, dose yourself daily with Absoluto.* How is it, then, that these diseases persist?'

'These were no physicians' prescriptions,' said the Philosopher. 'They were but the advertisements of the Patent Medicine Trust. All these sick people you saw were sick because they were poor, and so had to stint themselves in food. To pay for these pills and bottles they must stint their food again, and so again become ill.'

'I begin to understand your world,' said Cuchulain. 'While I was making these observations the Guardian of the tram came to me and held out his hand in a manner that I had at last come to know the meaning of. Can you get nothing in this world without money, my friend?'

'No,' said the Philosopher.

'Therefore,' said Cuchulain, 'I got up to leave the tram quietly, whereupon the Guardian laid hand on me as though to detain me. Nevertheless I smote him not, but, stopping, held his arm a moment, so that he paled and offered no further hindrance. Having dismounted from the tram, I accosted one who passed, asking him to direct me to Stoneybatter. Very quickly he gave me a description that I could not understand, and would have hurried away had I not detained him by the shoulder, saying: 'What, churl! is this your courtesy to a stranger? I have a mind to slay thee, but lead me on straight to Stoneybatter, and perhaps I may pardon thee.' Said the man of Dublin: 'What sort of a joker are you? Do you know who I am?' I said I did not.

'I am Solomon Beetlebrow,' quoth he, 'Minister of the Interior.' 'Your humble servant,' said I, bowing. 'But time presses, therefore lead on.' At that I took him by the ear, and in this wise he led me to Stoneybatter, but not without exciting some admiration in our course.'